S0-CLK-042

Official Licensed Product

Running Press Kids
Hachette Book Group
1290 Avenue of the Americas, New York, NY 10104
www.runningpress.com/rpkids
@RP_Kids

Printed in China

First Edition: July 2022

Published by Running Press Kids, an imprint of Perseus Books, LLC, a subsidiary of Hachette Book Group, Inc.
The Running Press Kids name and logo is a trademark of the Hachette Book Group.

Text written by JaNay Brown-Wood.
Illustrations by Rob Justus.
Print book cover and interior design by Marissa Raybuck.

Library of Congress Cataloging-in-Publication Data
Names: Brown-Wood, JaNay, author. | Justus, Rob, illustrator.
Title: Follow that line! : magic at your fingertips / written by JaNay Brown-Wood ; illustrated by Rob Justus.
Description: First edition. | New York, NY : Running Press Kids, 2022. | At head of title: Crayola. |
Audience: Ages 4-8. | Summary: Invites readers to use their fingers to follow the lines and create colorful works of art.
Identifiers: LCCN 2021013894 (print) | LCCN 2021013895 (ebook) | ISBN 9780762475025 (hardcover) |
ISBN 9780762475032 (ebook) | ISBN 9780762475049 (ebook) |
ISBN 9780762475100 (ebook) | ISBN 9780762475117 (ebook)
Subjects: CYAC: Art--Fiction. | LCGFT: Picture books.
Classification: LCC PZ7.B81983 Fo 2022 (print) | LCC PZ7.B81983 (ebook) | DDC [E]--dc23
LC record available at https://lccn.loc.gov/2021013894
LC ebook record available at https://lccn.loc.gov/2021013895

ISBNs: 978-0-7624-7502-5 (hardcover), 978-0-7624-7503-2 (ebook),
978-0-7624-7504-9 (ebook), 978-0-7624-7510-0 (ebook), 978-0-7624-7511-7 (ebook)

APS

10 9 8 7 6 5 4 3 2 1

FOLLOW THAT LINE!

Magic at Your Fingertips

Written by **JANAY BROWN-WOOD**

Illustrated by **ROB JUSTUS**

RP|KIDS
PHILADELPHIA

Do you want to know a secret?

You have magic in your fingers.

Want to see? Turn the page.

Take one finger and follow the line.

Whoa!

Now, take your thumb and follow this line.

See? Let's really get it going.

Hold your hands out and shake them three times.

Now wiggle your fingers five times, then turn the page.

Here we go!

Take your index finger and follow this line up and down

and up and down and up and down.

Look at that! You can make mountains.

Now take the tippy-tip of your pinky fingernail
and follow this line up, over, down, over.

And again: up, over, down, over, up, over, and down.

There! You can build buildings.
Turn the page again!

Take your thumb and press it down hard.
Now follow this line curving up and over, curving down and over, curving up and over, curving down and over,

curving up and over,

curving down and over.

Ah-ha! You can make waves!
Keep going!

Try this: follow each line with your two center fingers
and make five dots on the top of each line.
Line, dot, dot, dot, dot, dot. Line, dot, dot, dot, dot, dot.

Line, dot, dot, dot, dot, dot.

Wow! You can make flowers bloom. You're amazing.

Don't quit!

This time, spread all five fingers out wide

and follow this line up, then curve, then down.

You can create a rainbow!

But don't stop there. With all five fingers, keep going and follow the line down and curve, and around and around and around.

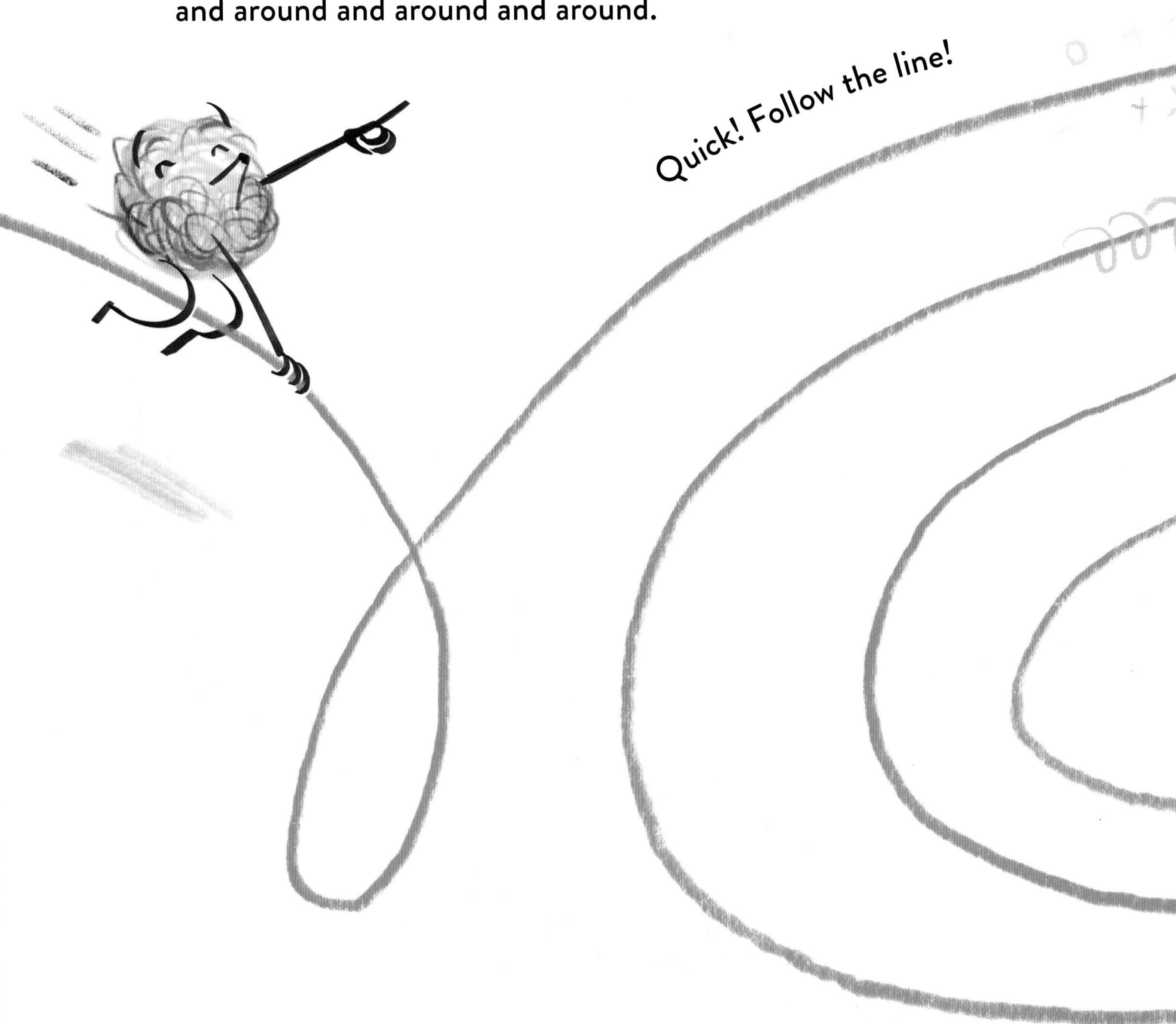

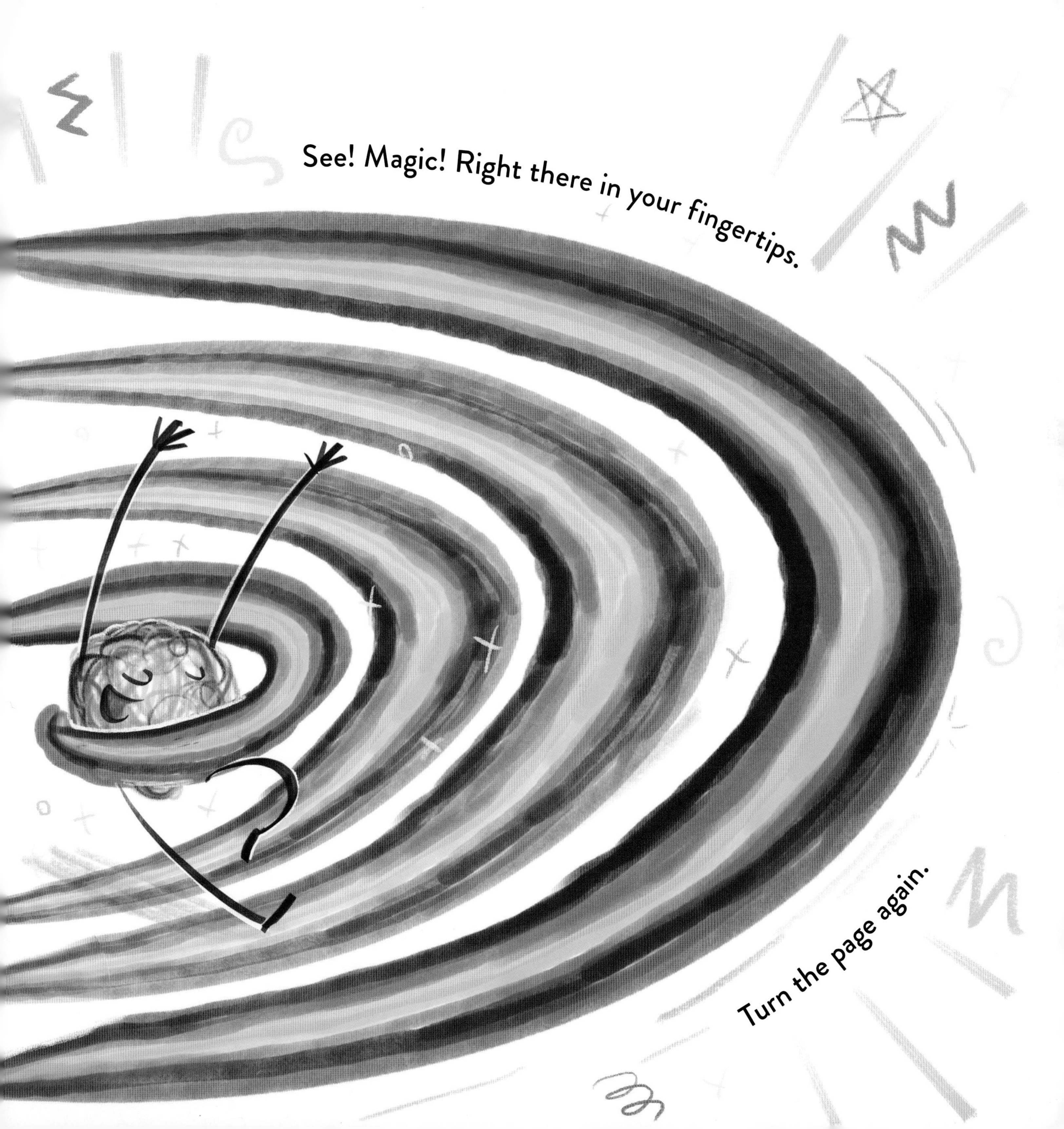
See! Magic! Right there in your fingertips.
Turn the page again.

Take all of your fingers on both of your hands and let them flow on the page.

Let them go this way and that way and this way and that.

Keep going! Now turn the page!

Amazing! Keep on going! Keep on flowing!

Turn the page again!

Wow! Magical!

With your fingers, you can follow the line . . .

. . . or just let your fingers flow.

You can create magic on the page
any way you choose!

Want to give it another go?
Grab some paper and some crayons,
markers, paints, and more!

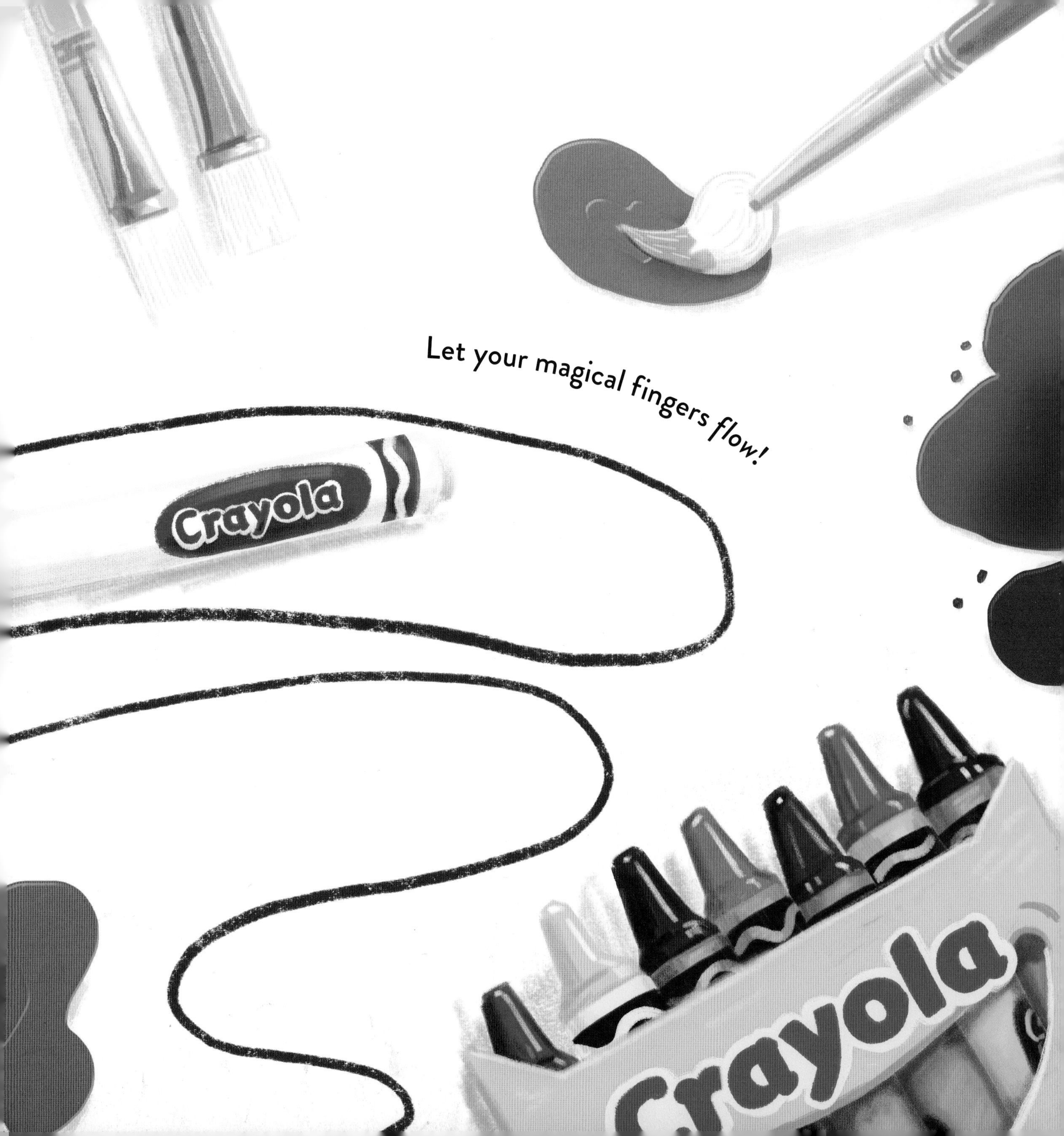

Let your magical fingers flow!

A NOTE FOR ADULTS

Providing children with opportunities to do art is so much fun! But it has other benefits as well. Arts and crafts projects can support creativity and fine-motor-skill development, especially in younger children.

You can use this book as a playful way to engage your readers with words and art. When reading the pages, use a sheet of paper to cover up the right page and gradually reveal the colorful artwork as the child follows the lines using their fingers. You can start doing this on page 11. Then, once you've read the whole book, offer the child their choice of art materials and watch the magic unfold!

JANAY BROWN-WOOD, PHD, is an award-winning children's author, poet, educator, and scholar. Her first children's book *Imani's Moon* won the NAESP Children's Book of the Year Award and was featured on *The Late Show with Stephen Colbert*, and her second book *Grandma's Tiny House: A Counting Story!* won the CELI Read Aloud Book Award. She also has several poems published in *Highlights for Kids*, *Highlights High Five*, and the poetry anthology *Thanku: Poems of Gratitude*. JaNay lives in California with her husband Catrayel, her daughter Vivian, and their two turtles. She enjoys writing for kids, spending time with her family, and spreading the word about the importance of diversity in children's literature, early literacy, and supporting the healthy development of children's. Learn more about her on her website www.janaybrownwood.com.

ROB JUSTUS is a former market researcher turned picture book author/illustrator and graphic novelist. He lives in Ottawa, Canada, with his family. To this day he's not sure which is his favorite Crayola: Red Violet or Magenta. His young son definitely prefers the taste of the orange ones.